GEORGE ROS

THE FOUR

FRIENDS FOR LIFE

BOOK ONE

ILLUSTRATOR : COCO

AuthorHouse™ UK
1663 Liberty Drive
Bloomington, IN 47403 USA
www.authorhouse.co.uk
Phone: 0800.197.4150

Published by AuthorHouse 11/21/2017

ISBN: 978-1-5462-8655-4 (sc)
ISBN: 978-1-5462-8654-7 (e)

Print information available on the last page.

Because of the dynamic nature of the Internet, any web addresses or links contained in this book may have changed
since publication and may no longer be valid. The views expressed in this work are solely those of the author and do not
necessarily reflect the views of the publisher, and the publisher hereby disclaims any responsibility for them.

authorHOUSE®

"We will be okay, I can hear sirens outside" Audrey said as the four children were standing close together in the corner of the classroom."

Try to stay calm. I'm not sure how long it will take them to get us out."

"Agrippa is bleeding" Brielle said. "Are you okay?"

"Yes, I'm fine thanks" Agrippa replied. "It's only a scratch."

"When I was younger I used to think you would have different coloured blood to me" Brielle told him; "then I found out that we might be different on the outside, but we are all the same on the inside."

"Typical girl" Basharat said raising his eyebrows.

"Hello!" a voice called from outside the classroom. "Are you children alright in there?"

"Yes, Miss Gregory" Basharat replied, recognising the voice. "We are fine."

"We will get you out as soon as we can" she told them. "Just keep calm and try to relax"

"We will" Audrey replied.

Brielle   Basharat   Agrippa   Audrey

The four children had been selected by the head teacher as they were the top students of their year on specific subjects. Miss Lisa Gregory was looking after them until the head teacher finished her morning duties.

Lisa knew every child in the school by name and face as she was responsible for looking after the library, updating the display boards around the school and taking photographs of the children for class portraits and individual school photos for their families.

She asked the four of them to meet in the classroom to organise how they could help children that were struggling in each of their specialised subjects.

Audrey was top of the group in Physical Education and particularly loved doing athletics and dance. She was an active girl and was ideally built for the sporting subjects she enjoyed.

Basharat was top of the group in English language and Communication and used to practice on his family when he was at home. His grandparents had only recently come to the country and were studying the language at night school.

Brielle was top of the class in Mathematics. She loved problem solving and working difficult sums out in her head without using a calculator.

Agrippa was top in Arts Education. He loved doing visual arts, drawing and painting. Some of his work was always on the display boards around the school.

They had only just sat down in the classroom when a lorry crashed into the school building.

The lorry driver had parked the lorry and gone to the newsagents nearby but forgot to apply his handbrake. The parked lorry came rolling down the hill straight into the school building.

Nobody was seriously injured but the structures had collapsed and trapped "the four" inside. Luckily the teacher was sitting at her desk by the door and the lorry ended up in between her and the four children but she couldn't get to them.

The emergency services couldn't risk trying to pull them out in case the ceiling come tumbling down on top of them, so they had to take it slowly organising how they were going to plan getting them out.

The children were quiet and motionless for a while before Audrey broke the silence.

"I can remember seeing you 3 around the school most days but I don't know your names"

"Agrippa" said the first boy

"Basharat" said the second

"I'm Brielle" said the other girl in the room

"I'm Audrey it's nice to meet you" she said with a smile "Where are your family from Agrippa?"

"A place called Burkina Faso in Africa" he replied "I was born in this country but my family still like to bring me up as an African boy"

"You are an African boy" Basharat told him "Where did you get a silly name like Agrippa from?"

"That's not a silly name" Brielle said "I've got a silly name"

"It was from when I was born" Agrippa told them "It means 'feet first' in African. My mum told me when I was born I came out upside down that's why they called me Agrippa"

The children chuckled.

So it wasn't a silly name after all.

"Where does your name come from Basharat?" Audrey asked.

"I've got three older sisters and my dad always wanted a boy" he explained. "So when I was born they called me Basharat which means "good news" in our language, so that's where my name came from."

"Wow" Audrey said "What about you Brielle do you know what your name means?"

"I do yes. My mum told me I was born early and was very very small" she said. "My parents didn't think I would survive. They said I was a fighter and after being in an incubator for 2 weeks I pulled through. So my parents called me Brielle which means 'God's Bravest Woman'"

"That's fantastic" Agrippa said. "So each of our names actually have a meaning in each culture."

"What about you Audrey?" Basharat asked her. "Does your name have a meaning?"

"It does actually," she said proudly "It means 'noble strength'."

"What is that supposed to mean?" Brielle asked.

"I don't honestly know" she told the others, "but it's not as good as your names."

They all started laughing.

Meanwhile, outside the collapsed school building, the Fire Chief in attendance, 'Jack Simmonds' who was in charge of the 'Incident Command Unit' and was also fully trained in managing building structural damage, surveyed the area. He was looking for visual signs of any affected part of the school building construction that could result in debris or masonry falling on the trapped children inside the building as the rescue and recovery effort was underway.

As it was going to be a long and slow process, he had to be sure none of his team moved anything that could result in any of the structure collapsing.

All of the staff from the school had been evacuated along with the majority of the children without injury.

As far as he was aware, there were only four children trapped inside the building and he didn't want to risk getting too close in case it weakened the structure.

The Head Teacher 'Adiva Hussain' asked Jack what was happening.

"We can't get too close until we assess the damage to the building" Jack replied. "The last thing we want to do is to make the situation worse and cause any further accidents."

"How long will it take?" asked the Head Teacher. Jack replied; "we can't take any risks, so at the moment, we cannot say; but I will keep you informed". "Can you confirmed how many people are still inside?"

"Yes" replied the head teacher "We've checked the register and accounted for all children and staff with the exception of four children"

"Are you sure there is definitely nobody else in the building?" asked Jack.

"Yes I'm positive" she said. "They were in the classroom not far from where the lorry crashed"

Lisa Gregory joined the two of them outside.

"I've spoken to the children that are trapped inside and it looks like they are fine" she told them. "They are laughing and joking together."

"That's great news" the Head Teacher said. "At least we don't have to worry about them panicking."

"Have their parents been informed?" Jack asked.

"Not yet" answered the Head Teacher "We had to make sure we checked everyone was out before we did anything else."

"Okay" Jack said "we are going to create a 'no go area' around the school grounds to keep people away."

"I will keep a regular check on the children to make sure they are alright" Lisa told them.

"Good idea" Mrs Hussain said. "We have to keep monitoring them constantly."

"Where can we direct the parents to go when they arrive?" Lisa asked.

"Into the space behind the wall on the right" Jack told her. "It's far enough away but close enough for them to see when the children come out".

She was relieved that he was confident in getting the children out safely.

The Police who had also arrived cordoned off the area. Most of the rescued children had already been collected by their parent or relative and taken home away from the scene.

Some of the parents of 'the four' children trapped in the building had arrived and were led into the area Jack had designated.

There was panic written over their faces and one of the women was sobbing as she watched what was going on around her.

Inside the collapsed classroom building, the children were calm but a bit worried. "Are you looking forward to Christmas?" Audrey asked the other three.

"We don't celebrate Christmas" Basharat told them "It's not an islamic tradition.

"No, we don't celebrate Christmas either" Brielle said "I'm from a jewish family".

"Wow. You don't know what you're missing" Agrippa said. "Christmas celebrations is fantastic".

"We have times of celebration too" Basharat told them, "and they are also fantastic".

"Same here", Brielle agreed. "We also celebrate other times of the year that other religions don't celebrate".

"So you two don't believe in God then?" Audrey asked.

Basharat and Brielle started to chuckle.

"Of course I believe in God but in our faith we worship differently to you", Basharat said.

"Us too" Brielle said "When we get out of here why don't we all spend a day at each other's houses and get to understand each of our cultures and beliefs".

"I think that's a wonderful idea" Audrey said "But will our parents agree to it?"

"I'm not sure" Agrippa said "My father can be funny letting others into our house".

"Mine too" Audrey agreed "I'm not sure what he believes in, he never talks about it".

"Do your parents go to church?" Basharat asked them.

"My parents don't" Audrey said. "But I know they believe in God as I sometimes hear them pray"

"My mother never misses church on a Sunday" Agrippa told them "My father goes sometimes but not every week; he was part of a traditional African religion".

"My parents follow their religious beliefs every day" Basharat said "They are true followers of Allah".

"I think it will be really interesting to find out about each other's faiths and why we believe in what we believe in" Brielle said. "That will be our mission when we finally get out of here".

"I agree" Basharat said.

"Me too" said Agrippa.

"And me" Brielle also agreed. "Why has it taken so long for them to get us out of here?"

"They are definitely still out there I can hear them" Agrippa told them. "But nobody has come close for a while".

"Maybe they have forgotten about us" Basharat said. "Why don't we all shout at once to see if they can hear us?"

"Good idea" Audrey said "After three"

"One" "Two" "Three"

"HELP!!!" all four of them screamed.

The building started to move and the four of them froze.

Jack heard the screams and saw the top of the structure move about 12 inches and STOP.

The parents of the children that had congregated in their designated spot grabbed each other and held tight.

"Please don't let anything happen to our children" Basharat's father said kneeling down.

The four mothers were panicking and started crying, they clung onto each other in a group. The other three dads felt numb and could only watch in despair.

They had seen each other around the school for years and never batted an eyelid to each other, but now they were united in worry and fear for their children.

"I can't believe it" Jack said to his colleagues.

"What?" one of them asked.

"Before the building moved we couldn't get into the structure without risking it collapsing", he told them. "But now the structures look as though they are supporting each other which will allow us to get in from one side".

"No way" his second in command said.

"Come on let's do it" Jack said, organising his crew and telling them exactly what to do. "Just one piece at a time guys, then wait, then another and so on."

"No problem boss" they all agreed.

When the building moved it frightened the children.

They started to pray at the same time in their own way.

They could hear the emergency crew moving the pieces of the building piece by piece and they all stared at each other and started to smile.

"It's amazing what can happen when we all pray to our own God" Basharat said "It looks like they heard us at the same time".

"So who's house is first on our learning trail?" Brielle asked "It can be mine if you want".

"Let's sort it out with our parents when we get out" Agrippa told them.

"I'm looking forward to it" Audrey said "I love learning new things".

The fire crew moved the last piece of the broken building away and that enabled the children to get out free.

Instead of running to their parents as you would have expected, they waited until all four of them were out and then, they held hands.

They raised their arms aloft and started smiling from ear to ear.

"WE'RE FREE" they shouted at the top of their voices.

Jack said "these children have just been freed after being trapped inside a building for almost 5 hours. You wouldn't think so would you?"

'The four' walked over to where their parents were standing holding out their arms.

The head teacher 'Adiva Hussain' and the chief fire officer 'Jack Simmonds' joined them.

"I think you four should be checked over by the ambulance crew" Mrs Hussain said signalling over to the paramedics.

"There's only Agrippa that has a graze on his leg" Brielle told them.

"Yes that's right" Basharat agreed "the rest of us are fine".

"Better to be safe than sorry" Jack told them "I can't believe you were all so brave".

"Absolutely", the head teacher said. "I couldn't believe it when you all came out smiling".

"We are friends for life" Audrey told them. "Would you like to tell your parents what we were talking about Brielle?"

Brielle explained what they had been talking about inside the building and told them she wanted her new friends to come to their house first.

Her parents agreed as did all the other three children's parents as well.

They exchanged numbers and addresses and said they would keep in touch to organise the visits to each of their homes.

The children were checked over by the paramedics and given the all clear apart from Agrippa who had a bandage round his grazed leg.

The families lived within 2 miles of each other so they decided that the parent of the child they were visiting would pick the other three up on the day.

Brielle would be first, then Basharat, then Audrey and finally Agrippa.

The children were excited and couldn't wait.

When the first day of the visits finally arrived, Brielle's father arranged to pick up the other three children at 5 o'clock in the evening

With the help of her mum, Brielle had prepared everything the day before. They only had to cook the hot food when they were almost ready to eat.

When the children arrived, the table was already set with their best cutlery, glasses and a 'bencher' a Jewish book containing blessings and songs used at mealtimes.

The room was set out exactly how it would have been when they celebrated 'Shabbat' a day of joy and rest.

This would start at sunset on a Friday until after sunset on a Saturday.

Her father and other relatives would go to where they worshipped at the 'synagogue' before coming home to the family.

They had placed a silver tray on the fireplace with candles inside silver candle holders ready to be lit when her mum was ready.

Brielle was very smartly dressed and guided her friends through the routines followed at the beginning of 'Shabbat'.

Her mother lit the candles and gave thanks to God while her father who was dressed casually with his 'kippah' a small hat worn on top of his head gave her a blessing from the bible.

Brielle then told her friends all about 'Shabbat' and what the family did at this time which included not using any electricity, and playing chess and other board games in candle light.

Brielle also told them about other festivals. The first was HANUKKA, the Jewish winter festival of light where they give presents to family members and friends. This lasts for 8 days and a candle is lit each day.

Next was SUKKOT; a Jewish harvest festival that lasts for a week and meals are eaten in a shelter made and decorated with leaves, branches, fruit and pictures.

Then PURIM, the Jewish carnival festival at the end of the winter where they have fancy dress parties, and perform plays. Presents are given especially to people that are either too old or ill to leave their homes.

Next, the PASSOVER a Jewish spring festival of freedom held at home where all the members of the family eat a special meal and play games, tell stories and sing songs together.

She also told them about her own personal coming of age ceremony known as 'Bar Mitzvah'. This would take place when she was 12 years old, in 4 year's time.

She explained about 'Kosher' foods that were eaten by the Jewish community, and explained that they only ate meat from certain animals, fish or birds.

Just as she finished her mum shouted to let her know that the food was ready to be served.

Her father reminded her that they usually had wine before the 'Shabbat' meal but on this occasion they would pass on that one.

Brielle's mum brought the food to the table and laid it out so that the children could help themselves.

They had Braided CHALLAH bread

Spicy BAZARGAN, Meat Stuffed KIBBEH, a big COUSCOUS ROYALE, and a juicy BRISKET for main course followed by dairy free flourless CHOCOLATE CAKE, Jelly filled SUFGANIYOT, Apple Cake and a Chocolate RUGELACH for afters.

The children loved it and almost ate the lot.

They all played games together before thanking her family for a lovely evening. They had learned a lot about the Jewish culture and enjoyed every minute of it.

Brielles father took them home at 8pm.

When they got home they told their parents all about their night with Brielle's family and were looking forward to the next evening out, next time at Basharat's home.

Basharats parents modelled their home on the Islamic culture of having privacy, modesty and hospitality.

His father picked up the other children on Thursday at 5pm.

Basharat met them at the door when they arrived.

"Can you please take off your shoes before you come in" he asked, adding that "when you enter the house can you also put your right foot first please".

He explained that it was all part of Islamic etiquette and custom, and when they took off their shoes could they take the left shoe off first – and when they left to put the right shoe back on first.

"I hope I don't get too confused" Agrippa said.

"Don't worry I will remind you" Basharat told him

He led them into a room opposite the main living area.

His mother had put cushions on the floor to make it more comfortable for the children while Basharat remained standing.

He was wearing a 'thobe' which is his traditional dress and felt very proud. Islamic Law says he must wear clothing that covers from the navel to the knee.

He told the girls that moslem women must cover themselves from head to toe with the exception of their hands and face.

Agrippa would wear similar to what he was wearing.

He explained that they worship their God – Allah in a mosque which has a large dome on the top of the building with a tower known as a 'minaret'.

"I've seen mosques when I've been in my dad's car" Brielle told them.

"Me too" Audrey said.

"On entering the mosque you have to take off your shoes and wash your hands, face, arms, head, ears and finally your feet before praying to Allah" he informed them. "We don't use a towel or tissues to dry ourselves it's not hygienic"; he continued to tell them more about the islamic faith.

When they pray, they must face towards 'Mecca' the holy city of Islam. The prayers are normally led by an 'Imam' and last for around 10 minutes.

He explained that men and women pray separately and the women worship in a different part of the mosque. There are also Koran schools in the mosque where children learn to read from the Qu'ran which is written in Arabic script and the pages are often beautifully decorated.

The words in the Koran were given to the prophet Mohammad by the angel Gabriel the messenger of Allah, and is full of rhythmic verses.

The Muslim custom is to pray 5 times per day, at dawn, midday, afternoon, sunset and before they go to bed.

The men always try to conduct their prayers at the mosque whereas the women may have other commitments and pray at home.

Even at home they need to remove their shoes and wash before prayers. They have 4 positions of prayer which are standing, kneeling, bowing with their hands on the floor and their head on the ground.

There are 5 things that a Muslim must do in their lifetime.

- Say there is no god but Allah

- Pray 5 times a day

- Give money to the poor

- Go without food during Ramadan the 9th month in the Muslim year

- Visit Mecca the holy city

Basharat finished the lecture on his religion and culture just when his mother called to say the food was ready.

The feast looked as magnificent as it was at Brielle's house.

Basharat asked them to join him in saying his traditional word of 'Bismillah' which means 'in the name of Allah.'

He also washed his hands in preparation to eat.

"We eat and drink using our right hand" he told them "If you prefer to use cutlery then let me know".

The children agreed to eat the same way as Basharat as they were in his home.

There was Naan breads and popadums with different sauces and dips to start.

Then there was Baida Roti, Chicken Biryani, Garlic Mustard Fish Fillet and Chicken Masala for main course followed by Ladies Delight with cream, Mohammabiah Strawberries cake and Raspberry yoghurt ice-cream.

"There's enough there to feed an army" Audrey thought

After they had finished their food they washed their hands and face before playing hide and seek and a couple of board games before it was time to go home.

Audrey really enjoyed the visits to her 2 new friends' houses to learn their habits and cultures, next it was her turn and she was feeling nervous.

She had the weekend to prepare herself as the other children were coming on Monday.

Her father picked the others up at 5pm as normal and Audrey was waiting at the door when they arrived.

She was wearing the cassock and surplice that she wore when she sang in the church choir, it looked lovely.

Her parents had a cross hanging up in the dining room with rosary beads hanging around it.

She escorted her friends into the room and asked them to sit down as she pressed play on the CD player.

Audrey sang the popular hymn known to the catholic faith 'Ave Maria'. It brought a tear to each of the children's eyes as she sang it so beautifully.

She explained that she was a practising catholic and believed that Jesus Christ was the son of god, and that the Holy Bible is the inspired, error free and revealed word of God.

She told them that her parents were not practising Christians but they did actually believed in God.

She attends the Catholic church every Sunday and believes that 'The Pope' who resides in Rome is the successor to St Peter whom Christ appointed to be the first head of the church.

She explained that as a catholic you're required to live a Christian life. Pray daily, participate in sacraments, obey the moral law and accept the teachings of Christ and his church. The minimum requirements are to attend mass every Sunday.

Audrey attends church with her grandparents as they are practising Christians, they even take her to choir practice she told her friends.

They believe in the birth of Christ as being a miracle to the Virgin Mary his mother and celebrate his birth at Christmas by giving and receiving presents with friends and family.

They also believe in giving to the poor and needy during this festive period.

Another time of major celebration which symbolises Jesus Christ's resurrection on the third day after his crucifixion is at Easter. This was when Mary Magdalene had gone to the tomb where Jesus was buried and found it empty and was told that he had risen.

Easter eggs are used as gifts to celebrate this occasion and some children even decorate boiled eggs and roll them down the hill as part of the celebration.

She explained that Christians believe that Jesus gave his life to enable us to eat and drink whatever we wanted so there were no restrictions on what food we ate.

Audrey's mother did consider her friends however and made sure that the food that they were having suited everybody's tastes.

For starters they had tomato soup with crusty bread or pate on toast.

Main courses consisted of roast beef, roast chicken or cod.

Her mother put dishes with an assortment of vegetables on the table so they could help themselves.

There was cauliflower, cabbage, green beans, peas, carrots and a great big bowl of chips.

After this for pudding they had apple pie, chocolate gateau, strawberries, ice cream and custard.

It was an unusual mixture for the children but as before they followed the traditions of their friends and ate the lot.

Audrey then got some of her favourite games out.

They played monopoly, scrabble, ker plunk and cards.

They hadn't laughed so much for a long time and there was even an attempt when the boys tried to cheat, but were caught out by the girls.

It was 8:30pm before Audrey's father had to more or less drag them away to go home, after another fantastic night had by them all.

Last to welcome their friends into his home was Agrippa.

He wasn't feeling comfortable as his father wasn't exactly over enthusiastic about welcoming strangers into his house. The only reason he eventually agreed was because his wife told him that it was for his son he was doing it and not for himself.

Also the fact that the other children's parents had welcomed Agrippa into their homes with open arms was another good reason for him to agree to it.

So he finally agreed and went on his mission to pick the other children up from their homes.

When they returned Agrippa was waiting to welcome them at the door. He was wearing the traditional boys Dashiki outfit and looked awesome.

Agrippa and his father welcomed them into their home and they all sat round a table. Agrippa started to explain his understanding of his religious beliefs.

His family believed in the African Traditional Religion which could be different to each family or tribe back in Africa itself.

His traditional beliefs are in their being a supreme creator, who he says could be any of the gods that the rest of his friends believe in, they believe in spirits who could be ancestors from the past, and they believe in black magic and in the use of traditional medicines.

He explained that they also believe that their ancestors have direct communication with god and send messages to them via the 'divinities', who are the link between the ancestors and the living.

He showed them his father's ceremonial mask that looked quite scary but was worn to protect him against bad spirits and to bring wealth and good harvests.

Agrippa also showed them photographs of when he went to a ceremony with his father in Africa and had all his body painted including his face.

The painting made him look like a skeleton but he was obviously having great fun with the look he had on his face.

His father also had a set of drums. They were used to greet visitors, honour spirits and celebrate happy occasions he told them. If Agrippa had practised enough he could have played a welcoming beat for them when they arrived into his home.

He told them that the drums were made out of antelope skins and the noise from the drum sounded like a leopard's snarl when you scraped powder across the drum skin with a drumstick.

Just as Agrippa was ready to try to play the drum, his mother popped her head around the door.

"Are you children ready to eat?" she asked

"Yes please" the children said almost all together.

"Wash your hands first please" Agrippa's mother told them.

The table was loaded with a mixture of all sorts of lovely food.

For starters or main course they were given the choices of Frikkadel, mandazi, samosa, shish taouk, sosatie and vetkoek.

Then for pudding they had the luxury of helping themselves to Malva pudding, guava ice-cream and milk tart.

When they had eaten as much as they could they were stuffed full to the brim.

After washing their hands and face they went back into the dining room to have another look at the mask and drums.

When they had finished playing and hearing some more stories from Agrippa's visit to Africa it was almost time to go home.

"Did you enjoy yourselves?" Agrippa asked.

"Yes that was excellent" Basharat answered

"It was indeed" Brielle confirmed.

"Can't we do it all again sometime?" Audrey asked them.

"Too much of a good thing takes the excitement away" Basharat said "Maybe we should do something different next time".

"Like what? " Asked Brielle.

"Adventures" Agrippa said "Why don't we go on some adventures together".

"One thing I've always wanted to do is to go to the safari park" Audrey told them.

"For me it would be camping" Basharat said.

"Oh no" Brielle commented; "think of all the bugs".

The children started laughing out loud.

"We've got plenty of time to plan ahead before the next holidays" Audrey told them "We will decide what to do then".

'The Four' go on adventure" Basharat said smiling "I can't wait".

"See you soon in BOOK 2 – Team Work"

Lightning Source UK Ltd.
Milton Keynes UK
UKRC02n1135230118
316673UK00004B/22

9 781546 286554